Little Sips from a Southern Punch Bowl ...

Musings, Ironies and Tributes

By **KATHRYN HILL**

Printed in the United States of America

ISBN: 979-8-9904386-0-6

TABLE *of* CONTENTS

Introduction..7

1. Traveling Porch Swings 9

2. A Good Reputation.. 13

3. Reflections on Life 17

4. Amazing Friends 21

5. Southern Preachers 25

6. Girlfriends...29

7. Being Southern 33

8. Christmas Magic 39

9. What Do I Want for Christmas?...................... 45

10. Letters 47

11. Listening Is Not Reading 55

12. Computers & Writing 59

13. Home Healthcare 61

14. Hospital Tips 67

15. BOGO!.. 73

16. The Great Garage Sale 81

17. An Attempt to Simplify 87

18. An Economy of Words 91

19. Remembering 9-11-2001................................. 97

20. The Deconstruction of the American Male.......... 103

21. I'm So Sorry You're Hurting 109

22. Art History of the Wiener Dog 113

23. Beyond the Clouds 117

24. The Last Time 121

25. Death and Heartache 125

26. Reincarnation 127

27. Fate & Destiny 131

Thank for you for
a wink and a smile.

INTRODUCTION

I bought a blank sketch book a few years ago with the intent that I would fill it with a few notes and little stories about family, friends, travels . . . maybe throw in some special photographs, a few life lessons . . . things that I would like to remember and revisit from time to time.

Really in no particular order – just random – like life.

What I have learned is that life is too short not to enjoy every day and if you are fortunate enough to share it with someone you love, it's even better.

— *Kathryn Hill*

Traveling Porch Swings

Back in the mid-1960s, there was a group of young women bound by their love for their community and they formed the Women's Service Association of Rockdale County.

While none of the original members are here today, the legacy of the WSA still exists. The WSA continued with the next generation of girlfriends. Today, now mostly grandmothers, with years of stories to tell - their lives intertwine like strands in a rope.

They travel together as a sisterhood – to celebrate pure, undiluted, non-judgmental fun.

When they travel together, they laugh for three or four days solid; taking over a small area of a restaurant or a once quiet little bar. They laugh until exhaustion sets in. Their unofficial motto: *"I love the nights I can't remember with friends I can't forget".*

Recently the friends traveled to Callaway Gardens in Pine Mountain, Georgia, reprising their Spring break adventure – a traveling tribe of women impervious to deaths, divorce, sickness, relocation and time. Not once in the years have the friends, as a group, decided to pass on their getaway.

In the beginning, back a few years ago when their traveling began, the trip was going to be just a quick weekend adventure to New York City. Over time, the trips have become less of an adventurous getaway weekend and more social. It's not a requirement to go to a faraway place. They are golfers, hikers, runners, shoppers and readers. But on these trips, they are more about porch swings than golf swings. They would be happy just around the corner.

Typically they travel together in a caravan of two or three cars, maximizing the time they have to tell stories and giggle like school girls. They even talked about hiring a limo with a driver just to visit the wineries of north Georgia. One can only imagine "Driving Miss Daisy" times eight.

They cry with each other, advise one another, praise and lift up their friend and each holds the other dear to their heart.

They taste test unusual foods, try on different clothes when shopping, listen to each other's stories, laugh until tears run down their legs. If there's a design to their hijinks, it's to create instant stories – stories that will go down easy five years from now with a glass of wine and a soft breeze on their face.

*"I love the nights
I can't remember
with friends
I can't forget".*

A Good Reputation

I've been fortunate to meet many people in my life and I wish I could remember them all - good and bad. Especially those that have been kind to me and I just simply overlooked it at the time.

One such person I recall with respect, admiration and great fondness was a true southern gentleman. A lawyer named Bobby Stringer. Bobby, and his "coffee group" as they called themselves, would meet every morning before the day's daily business would begin at some little restaurant just off the square in Decatur, Georgia. The local jeweler, Tom Moody, was always seated next to Bobby; never across from him but always just to Bobby's right.

I remember that Bobby spoke with the slightest of accents; one that sounded to me as a weeping willow whispering in the late afternoon. Calm and quiet – you could hear its long thin branches as they touched the ground when the air stirred them.

A bit of wisdom I will always remember is when Bobby spoke to me about the meaning of a good reputation. He actually wrote it to me in a letter that I will cherish for the rest of my life.

He said that a good name and reputation in the community is something to be called upon and used when needed and necessary. That the longer this reputation is maintained, then the more powerful it is when time comes for it to be used. Otherwise, there might not be any benefit to one who does have a good name and reputation.

If it is ever needed at some time in the future, that person should be given the opportunity to use the good name and reputation stored by them through the years in order for it to be valuable.

I liken a good reputation to a well. We fill it with our actions and we draw from it when we need to use it.

Thank you for your good actions toward me, Mr. Stringer. What a wonderful reputation you had in your community.

3

Reflections on Life

My birthday will be here soon, just like it has for at least the other thirty-nine years, and I'm a little depressed this year. Don't get me wrong. It is better to have one more than *not* to have one, but even so, it seems like there is not an upside this year.

Ice cream is bad for my good cholesterol and good for my bad cholesterol, the smoke detector in the kitchen will go off because there are so many candles on the cake, and I have to listen to people tell me that I don't look my age. That is true, by the way, I don't look my age – I think in the mornings I look much older than my age. Family will do that to you, but that's another story.

I will say this for birthdays, however. They are good days to pause and reflect on what I have learned during my time on this earth. So this year I am taking a moment to reflect upon some of the truths I have discovered while making this journey through life. I wouldn't call what follows the wisdom of the age;

it is not that wise and I am not *that* old. It is more like a few facts I have found over time and some observations I have had the opportunity to make. Now that I have the benefit of hindsight, I am willing to share this knowledge with everyone. So, here goes.

The checklist of "things to do" has no end. It will go on forever. The more channels you get on the television, the less likely it is that you will find something to watch. If the price for the entire meal is advertised at $5.00 including the drink and dessert – keep driving and do not stop there.

People don't usually change their minds about politics, religion, healthcare or onions and garlic. Just because the light is on does not mean that cash register lane is open. Antiques are for the most part just old junk with positive attitudes and good marketing.

Sometimes, the experts don't know what to do either. Telephone bills are unreadable, so don't feel bad if you can't make heads or tails out of yours. Heck, I'm not even sure who my carrier is these days. The grass actually is sometimes greener on the other side, but then again I wonder what their water bill is each month. The person on the back of a motorcycle never looks as happy as the person driving it – I guess what they say is true, "If you're not the lead dog, the view never changes."

There is not an "any key" on your computer keyboard. Before you get too excited at the half-price sale, remember that the merchandise was originally marked up at least one hundred percent to start with. You can always eventually get there from here. As it turns out, everything is bad for you, but not quite as bad as researchers once thought. Researchers are bad for you.

Coach seats on an airplane are examples of cruel and unusual punishment and as such they certainly violate the Eighth Amendment of the Constitution. Bottled water has actually caught on – who would have thought that? Calling it "art" doesn't always make it art, no matter the price tag.

If the button is not labeled, do not push it. Unless your name is Jacques or Luca and your weight is less than one hundred pounds, do not buy a Speedo.

While you may be right, the eighteen-wheeler is bigger. Do not ever try and beat the train. Do not mix checked shirts with striped trousers if you are a man. The back of your debit card is a bad place to jot down your PIN. Always pay the plumber – no matter how much it is just pay the bill.

Fish never know if it's raining or not. Twenty year paint will not last twenty years so you might as well buy the cheap stuff.

Well, there you are. And if you found any of these observations to be life-changing, you are not getting out enough.

4

Amazing Friends

To write about the accomplishments of others brings a sense of pride and pleasure. It eases my soul that I am able to write of rare gifts.

My life is touched by amazing people – by many wonderful women that offer distinctive gifts – offer friendship.

There is a tireless intimacy among women that are friends – an unbelievable strength and lastingness. I do often wonder what the source of that creation is.

When we get together we talk about food and wine, weight and exercise, clothes, books, family and characters we meet on our journey through life. You should join us one day, quietly of course – just pull up a chair, sit down in a corner - eavesdrop on our conversations. You would walk away as amazed as I always am when the talking is over and the day draws to a close. I love the voices that tell those great stories.

The character of my female friends is judged by how they comport themselves in daily life. They become a role model for everyone around them – their friends, their family and their community. They feel everything – elation, despair, wonder and failure. They carry themselves with immense pride.

There are few people whose very existence makes life bearable for the rest of us – for reasons of grace, wisdom and understanding. The women that I hold dear, those that I cherish their friendship, are among such people.

5

Southern Preachers

It started with a photo that I saw.

In 1950s black and white, there is a man in his rolled-up shirt sleeve, standing in a little river with water up to his waist. He is wearing a white dress shirt with sleeves rolled up.

Some called him "Preacher". Folks around town called him Howard. His children called him Daddy.

Benjamin Howard Nethery was a multi-tasking preacher, meaning that he owned a little grocery store, he painted houses, he farmed through the week and then stood in a pulpit for the Lord on Sundays. Every night, he came home, headed straight to the bathroom and scrubbed his hands for dinner. His hands always carried callouses; those callouses followed him to his grave.

In the memories of many, oftentimes Reverend Nethery, waded into the water to test the depth. In the hills of middle Tennessee, then and still now, little Baptist churches use natural resources to baptize the newly-saved.

Once after pulling a little boy out of the water, the child shouted, "Jesus has washed away all my sins!"

Later, I saw a couple of other photos where several folks were lined up, waiting for their turn to hold their noses and hear Preacher declare, "I baptize thee in the name of the Father, the Son, and the Holy Ghost."

This image was lingering sweetly in my mind one afternoon as I passed the table in the library. There is always a stack of books scattered about. My eye caught a similar black and white photo of a river baptizing on the cover of "Appalachian Mountains Religion: A History."

I picked it up to flip through it. I knew immediately where I had gotten it. It was a gift from my preacher long ago. Steve Moreno. He could be polarizing, but he was also a former Marine who meant business and stuck to doing what was best for the people he represented.

When I was 18, I heard his booming voice from the pulpit of Loganville Methodist Church. He listened intently to my questions and my conversations about life, the war in Viet Nam, youth and marriage. In common, we shared many things: love of God, our country, and most especially, our little community. He and his wife, Delores, became my friends.

From time to time, he'd send a handwritten note, saying something like, "Oh, how proud you make me. You keep sticking up for your beliefs."

When he left the ministry, he wrote a remarkably powerful, compassionate note. I keep it in a very special little box with memories from long ago.

Leafing through this book, I discovered a bonus: Steve had underlined sentences and placed stars and check marks by particularly interesting facts such as river baptizing, although that's not what the Methodist do, it was very symbolic to him and brought many mountain preachers back to his mind.

"Mountain religion is a religion of the heart." He underlined that in red.

I smiled, thinking of these two men, the truths they held tightly and the children they raised.

For both, it was this simple: Everything was black and white.

Girlfriends

I sat on the front porch one afternoon with my mother and she said, "Don't forget your girlfriends. No matter how much you love your husband, you are still going to need girlfriends.

Remember to go places with them now and then; and do things with them, even when you don't really want to".

Women supporting and relating to other women is our responsibility and our gift.

What a funny piece of advice, I thought. Hadn't I recently gotten married? Hadn't I just gotten married and joined the world of couples? I was married, for goodness' sake, not a girl anymore that need friends – I had a husband now.

But I listened to my mother.

I kept in contact with my girlfriends and even found some new ones along the way.

As the years passed quickly by, I gradually came to understand that my mother really knew what she was talking about.

Here is what I know:

Girlfriends know when you need help. They bring pizza and wine, scrub your bathroom or help pack your boxes when they know you're moving away from them.

They keep your secrets.

They give advice whether you ask for it or not.

They don't always tell you you're right, but they usually tell you the truth.

Girlfriends still love you, even when they disagree with you.

They laugh with you for absolutely no reason at all.

They don't keep a calendar of who hosted the last get together.

Girlfriends will celebrate with you for your son or daughter or grandchildren.

They are there for you in an instant, and when the hard times come, and they will come, they are there.

They listen when you lose a job or a friend.

They listen when your children break your heart.

Girlfriends listen when your parents' minds and bodies fail.

Girlfriends bless our lives.

When I began this adventure, I had no idea of the incredible joys or sorrows that would be ahead of me. Nor did I know how much I would need a friend . . . I'm sure glad I listened to at least one piece of advice from my mother.

Being Southern

Every now and then, a non-native will ask me what's so special about being a Southerner.

Well . . . everything!

We're colorful for one. We don't just eat a biscuit, we eat a cathead biscuit. We're obsessed with large reptiles, quality pine straw and oddly shaped fruits and vegetables.

I remember a few years back when I was doing a bit of photography, I was taking pictures in my parents' backyard of some of mother's tomatoes. A friend of theirs stopped by and proceeded to tell me to be sure and get a picture of one nearly ripe tomato because it was shaped like "male geeny-talia". These, and photos of five foot long rattlesnakes always seemed to make the front page of every local newspaper in the South.

Southern men believe that if you shoot something, anything – it doesn't matter what it is – you must tie it on the hood of your car or truck and parade it around town. You can call that disgusting but they call it dinner.

Southern women live by a simple set of rules that keeps the chaos at bay:

- Never wear sweatpants in public. (Actually you should really never wear them in private either.)

- Always keep a "funeral casserole" in the freezer (or cheese biscuits in my case).

- Always say "The" Wal*Mart out of respect.

- Never use a toothpick in the restaurant parking lot because sure as you do, somebody's going to remember you were the Soperton Guano Queen back in 1970 and they'll talk about how you've just let yourself go.

- Always make sure to have a burial plot in the "good" section of the cemetery or have the good sense to lie about it and say that you do.

- Always wear "big hair" for important events such as the Georgia home football games or when Paula Deen shows up for a cooking class.

༈ Avoid using "party" as a verb unless cousins from Tennessee are visiting, then it's okay to say "par-tay".

Southerners may move away from their roots, but a Southern man will always call his father *"Deddy"*, no matter if he's a Co-Cola executive who has given up grits for polenta and catfish for sushi.

I don't care how much a transplanted Southerner thinks he's left that foot-washing, fire-baptized, turnip green eating world behind, if *"The Devil Went Down to Georgia"* comes on the radio, he will holler "turn it up" and wonder out loud for the umpteenth time why *"Free Bird"* isn't the national anthem.

Over the years, I have grown to appreciate what it means to be a Southerner. We're proud and quirky and stubborn and funny. We don't just say we like turnip greens, we say that we've eaten so many we have to wear kerosene rags tied around our ankles to keep the cutworms off!

We don't just say we've caught a big fish, we say it was so big we had to use a hoe to clean it and then we sold the scales for dinner plates at the local flea market.

We are most fond of saying that if we had two homes – one above the Mason Dixon Line and the other in hell, we'd rent the one up north and live in hell.

We never turn off the television, unless a body is lying in state in the living room.

We understand that y'all is the most perfect word in the English language. "Do y'all want to keep y'alls forks for y'allses' peach cobbler?"

We're proud to be from the land of kudzu and honeysuckle, lightning bugs, tent revivals and sugar sweet tea.

8

Christmas Magic

Several years ago my son, Stephen, was very clear at Christmas about how their daughter's first Christmas and each one in the future would be spent: "We're not going to do Santa Claus, we're teaching our daughter why we celebrate Christmas and it's not for the presents."

What?

He rattled off his indictments of Christmas, starting with religion, followed by commercialism and then he started on the pure physics of the entire enterprise.

"There is no way we are going to start out with this Santa foolishness," he spouted. "We're not going to let her believe all this Santa stuff and then one day figure out we've been lying to her! She'll realize one day there's no Santa and think we were just liars. How stupid is that, thinking that one man can visit every house in a single night. How does he get into the houses with no chimneys? There's not a single animal book around that even mentions flying reindeer. And, we don't want her to think being fat is okay either."

How sad I felt when I heard his ramblings. Perhaps a more sensible parent (or grandparent) would have voiced an opinion at that time but I just listened and then did what I always do – I went shopping for more Christmas presents.

This Christmas, I watch with excitement not only little Emily but her sister, Anna. This past weekend as I closed the flue on the fireplace, Emily asked why I was doing that, "Santa won't be able to get down the chimney if you close it, Mimi." I assured her I would open it on Christmas Eve because I didn't want to miss my visit by Santa because I had the chimney blocked!

As I remember my son's mandate from a few years ago about the "facts" of Christmas, I watch these little girls with intrigue as they touch the ornaments on the tree and point out their favorites. It's always easier to do that when you're the grandparent and not the parent.

I recall a book I read many years ago by G. K. Chesterton. It was about faith and religion and magical things. It was a period in my life when I was seeking to learn about such things and try to put my logical thought processes aside for the illogical. All things that cannot be explained.

"Orthodoxy" was written more than a hundred years ago. It attempted to explain the unexplainable. Not whether the

Christian faith can be believed but of how Chesterton came to believe. Chesterton offered no real authority in his book, only his philosophy, his path to God and his belief in magic. Perhaps God *is* simply a magician.

Magic *has* been around forever – just like God. It gets under the skin of many people – atheists, scientists, lawyers – logical thinkers. Children's stories always contain magic; they are written as fairy tales. I believe that Santa Claus is the ultimate fairy tale but one that endures all ages – not just limited to children. I suspect that fairy tales and Santa prepare us to embrace the greatest fantasy of all and to promote "anti-scientific" thinking.

While many are puzzled because children will eventually abandon Santa, they keep believing in God. How can that be? We don't see Him anymore than we see Santa!

I think that Christians seek to reason their way to God. They go on archaeological digs, they verify their finds, and they place them on exhibit to "prove" they are actually godly things. Others dress up for that morning service, pass the collection plate in the name of God and build mega churches – what happened to the simple stable and the Star? Gosh, they didn't have microphones and airplanes with crosses painted on the tails and preachers on cable TV.

I suppose all that's fine but it seems to miss a fundamental point that Chesterton wrote of. To believe in God is to believe in mystery. In magic.

I believe that it is essential to preserve a small, inviolate space in the heart of my granddaughters. A space where it is free to believe impossibilities exist; a place that only by looking through the eye of magic can you see God. After all, He did turn water into wine – that's pretty magical!

How does one see invisible things? Only people raised on fairy tales can make sense of that. It belongs in a world where magic glasses can illuminate hidden things – rabbit holes turn into wonderlands.

I know that one day Emily and Anna Grace will figure out the Santa secret but I'm hopeful that the magic never leaves them. The magic of mystery and faith. That's why I'm not giving up on this Santa thing; not everything we believe can be proved or disproved by science. We believe in impossible things, and in unseen things, beginning with our own souls and working outward. It's a pretty delicate thing, believing. Preparing them to let go of one magical, mysterious believe but yet wanting them to hold onto another – the magic of God.

I read online this year's new words for 2009 and saw they were dropping words like "dwarf", "elf" and "devil" from the Oxford University children's dictionaries and will make room for "blog", "Euro" and "biodegradable". Wow! Not just a blow to the

English language but what's a fairy tale without an elf?

Well, I'm hanging in there with Santa, knowing that my grandchildren will gradually exchange fairy tales for faith. Their parents are teaching them about faith and Jesus and the "reason for the season". I'm sure of that — just not sure of their Santa teachings.

In our house there's no shame in believing the impossible exists. I hope our home is always filled with fairy tales and rabbit holes. I hope that the magic sprinkled across the pages of those fiction books will linger in the hearts of our children and grandchildren forever.

Now, where's the note I wrote for Santa to go with his cookies and milk?

9

What do I want for Christmas?

I want to sit back and admire the life you have.

I'm very proud of it.

I want you to spend your time and money making a better life for you and your family.

I want to see you happy and healthy.

So when I'm asked, "What do I want for Christmas?"

I can honestly say "nothing" - because you've already given me my gift all year through.

Merry Christmas and know I love you.

Written for my boys, December 2017

10

Letters

Letters vs. L-e-t-t-e-r-s

There seems to have been an art that is lost – the one of writing letters.

I love writing letters – and notes – to those that are near and dear to me. I try to always write thank you notes as I think they are important; not that the giver expects it but my goodness, if someone takes the time to offer you a gift or send you flowers (or sometimes just pick up the phone and give you a call), I believe that's worth a "thank you". Again, a lost art.

Letters take complete words – with punctuation, proper spelling and a little thought behind the contents. Today we send emails or text – all cryptic with whatever letter, symbol or number that pops into our head. Most often without much thought.

DC the 18 1878

Benton City Texas

Mr John L Green Dear uncle
it is with much pleasure that
I attempt to answer your kind
letter wich come safe to hand
and found me blest with good
helth hoping these lines may
reach you in due time and find
you blest with the same Well
uncle I dont know that I have
much to rite that would interres
you people complain of hard
times Well uncle as for pretty
girles thare is plenty of
them out hear I am not married
yet I have taken considerbul
liking to som of the girles chris
mus is clost at hand I think
that I will have A nice time
with the girles uncle I have plenty
of hard work to do I alwayes
found plenty of that to do

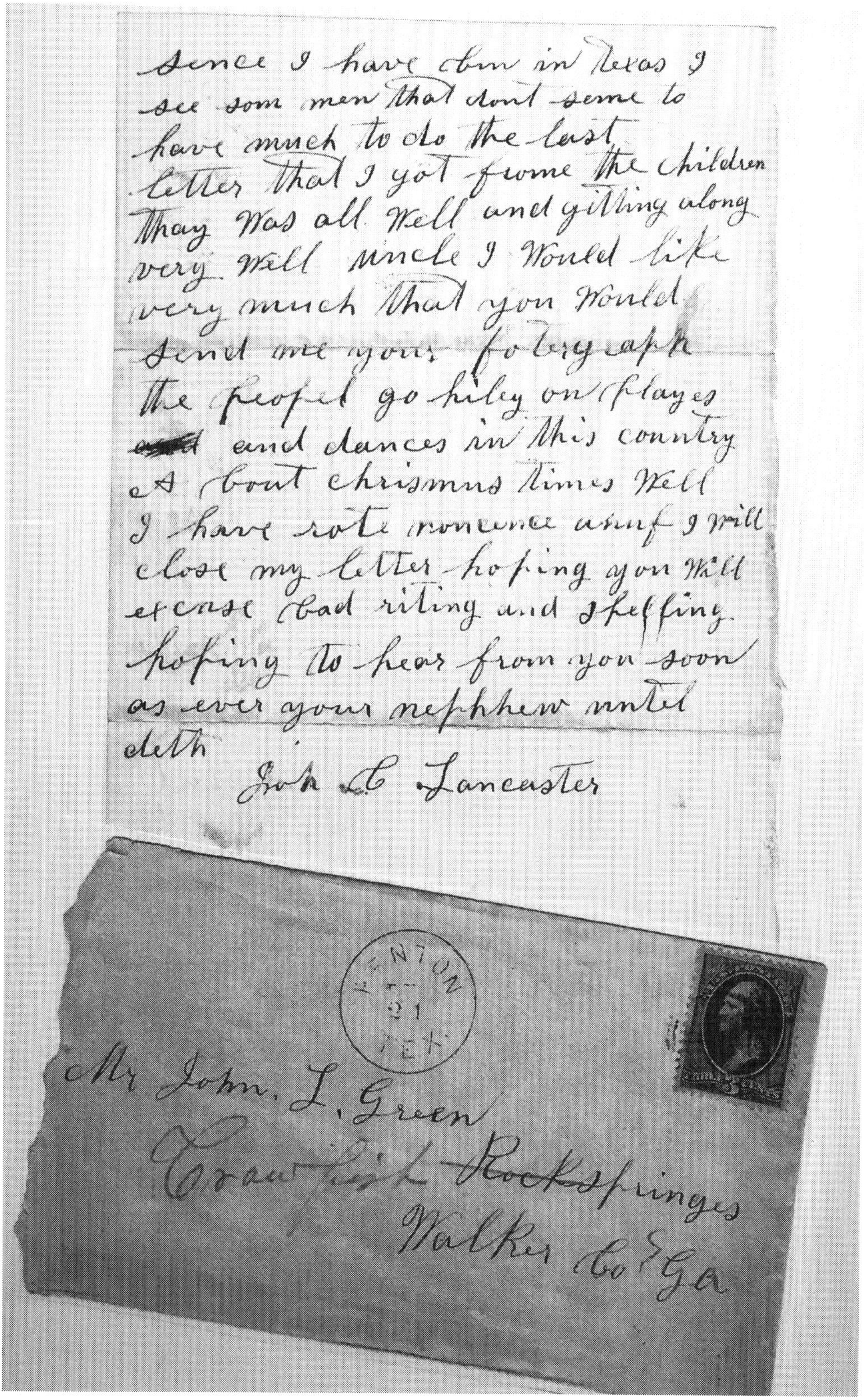

since I have ban in Texas I see som men that dont seme to have much to do the last letter that I got frome the children thay was all well and gitting along very well uncle I would like very much that you would send me your fotergraph the peopel go hiley on playes and dances in this country A bout chrismus times well I have rote nonceence anuf I will close my letter hoping you will excuse bad riting and speffing hoping to hear from you soon as ever your nephhew untel deth

Jno L C Lancaster

Mr John L Green
Crawfish Rockspringes
Walker Co Ga

Ringgold, Ga.

January 3rd, 1910.

Mrs. Martha Bilbo!

    Dear Friend-

        I will again write you a few lines as I have a cliping from the Walker County mesenger about Mr.Bilbo that I want to send you.
    You may have seen it,I will send it anyway because it is a good piece.
I hope you had a nice time Christmas and a happy New Year.Evrything was quiet here during Christmas it was so cold.
There was not anything to do at Post Oak,there was a Christmas-Tree at Peavine but there was'nt many there;it was Christmas Eve night when it rained so hard.

        Ottis says he would like awfull well to see Mrs. Bilbo.
We have missed you and Mr.Bilbo very much During Christmas and it seemes so lonesome down there at the house now,as there is no one lives there.
    Will close for this time wishing you and your friends all well,
        Iam yours Respt.

January 5, 2016

Dear Kathryn,

I wanted to share a brief story with you regarding the last time I saw Charlie. It was the nineteenth of October, and we had a great visit together with Julie in hygiene. His check-up was very good, and I personally thought Charlie looked terrific! He was in great spirits, and thanked me for my care through the years.

As I recall, Charlie's appointment was from 3:00 - 4:00 p.m., and I was surprised to see him sitting outside the office on one of the upstair sofas in the lobby about 4:15 or 4:20. I took him a bottle of water, sat beside him, and asked him if he was waiting for you to pick him up. He told me, "no," that he was just struck by the beauty of the turning leaves of our office park maple trees, and of how the late afternoon sun had illuminated the beautiful artwork (of Steffan Thomas) in our lobby. He said he just wanted to sit there for a while and "take it all in." He commented that "we rush through life, and miss so much beauty around us every day." I quietly sat with him for several minutes, finally thanked him for his long friendship, gave him a hug, and went back to work. When I turned back to look at him through the closed glass door of the office, he was still sitting there, looking very much at peace.

Thanks for sharing your wonderful husband with me these many years. Charlie will always remain in my heart as a class act, a true southern gentleman, and a complete professional.

Much love,

Wayne

Poppa Hill,

I know you have taken your last flight from this world.
I bet even you were amazed at the lights of _heaven_ when you made your "final approach".
I wish I could have seen your face when Jesus said "Welcome home my good and faithful servant."

Poppa Hill - you are one of the kindest souls I have ever known.
Thank you for taking such great care of my mother.
You were her Knight in Shinning Armour.
I will miss the joyful spirit you brought into our lives, and the way you would not let any of us leave before you got your hugs.
While my earthy body weeps because of your departure; the Holy Spirit inside of me rejoices knowing the LORD has called you home.
I LOVE YOU and I WILL SEE YOU AGAIN.

A note that you would actually put in the post telling someone you love them, now becomes in today's world an artless text of some emoji that says, "I ♥ u". *How sincere, how romantic.*

Now there is credit in writing emails or sending texts. One terrific thing about email is its immediacy. A conversation can be had – a decision made, a plan refined – in a matter of minutes, no matter where in the world the two parties happen to be.

A letter, by contrast, always arrives from the past. There is a waiting - a forced patience - built into the mechanics. You wait for a letter to arrive. You wait for a reply. In the time it takes for the letter to reach its destination, anything can happen: minds can be changed, lives lost, loves discovered.

This sense of duration also gives a sense of where the writer was, in both space and time: I am sitting at the kitchen table; I am in the garden; I am at a sidewalk café in Milan. In that sense, a letter is more "composed" than an email.

But the differences between letters and emails are just that - differences. One is not better or worse than the other. In many ways, the differences are cultural, generational if you will – they shift away from reading in print to reading on screen.

Sending a letter is the next best thing to showing up personally at someone's door. I do not know of a richer and more satisfying way of getting to know a person than through letter writing.

Words seem to flow onto paper very easily for me. Ink from your pen touches the stationary, your fingers touch the paper, and your lips have sealed the envelope. Something tangible from your world travels through machines and hands, and deposits itself in a loved one's mailbox. Your letter is carried inside their home as though it were an invited guest. The paper that was setting on your desk, now sets on another's. The recipient handles the paper that you handled. Letters create a connection that modern, impersonal forms of communication will never approach.

I have held on to letters for years, actually a few that I cherish are centuries old and tell stories of my ancestors from times that we can barely imagine. Letters not only serve a purpose in the here and now, they also stand as historical records, giving us an incomparable window into the past. I hope that whenever my children or grandchildren come across these old letters that they feel transported back into another time and place just as I do. There is a legacy in the power of letters. The collection of letters that I have is one of my most treasured possessions.

There are two letters that I read on a regular basis – they keep me grounded and they remind me of things that are important in my life. They can never be replaced and will always be in my memory - not only because of their content but the fact that two men took the time to sincerely write them.

11

Listening is Not Reading

Reading is one of the great pleasures of in my life. I am not certain about having someone read to me though. Not everyone can read aloud in a way that makes others want to listen, but the market for that skill keeps growing through audiobooks. Charlie was a big fan of audiobooks long before they became popular – he would rent cassettes from the local library and listen to them on the way back and forth to the airport.

We read books, either to ourselves or aloud. We listen to someone else read. Both can be delightful experiences. The experiences are similar, but different and the difference is important. They require different kinds of concentration.

No one should drive a car while reading a book (although I've seen it done by several people driving on Atlanta interstates – truly, I have – newspapers or books propped on the steering wheel!). Research indicates that most audiobooks are heard in vehicles. Many audiobook consumers listen while engaged in physical activity of some kind – walking, exercising, cleaning house or other chores.

My mother and her mother were master story tellers and tale-telling was a common occurrence while growing up. Occasionally, I wondered why reading seemed more inviting than watching a movie. My curiosity faded but the enjoyment of reading remained.

Whenever a book is recorded and published as an audiobook it becomes a new piece of work imbued with personal interpretation reflected in the narrator's voice. The production company, sound engineer and others add something to the recording that did not come from the author. When listeners hear the book, they are not reading the author's work but experiencing anew.

While we read and process the meaning of the written words, in our heads we are visualizing and hearing sights, actions and sounds. Listening requires us only to process meaning and sound. The outcome is less than the full senses allow us to imagine.

Reading is pleasurable and fulfilling in a special and personal way. When reading in silence and solitude, we draw upon personal experience and imagination to interpret the world the author offers in the written words.

12

Computers & Writing

There is an astonishing wealth of information on the devices we carry around with us – a wealth that should be celebrated. To me, I would prefer to read a single article or book with the kind of deep, measured concentration that seems to come more naturally with print.

A printed book stays on your shelf, and can be bookmarked by scribbling important missives in the margins or important passages can be highlighted; a printed book can be flipped through and shared. I know, I know - these things are all possible with digital devices and they may come naturally to some people – just not to me.

13

Home Healthcare

Medicine has come a long way in my lifetime. It seems like every time I open a newspaper or go online, I read of yet another advance in medical technology or another scientific breakthrough that will help us to live longer. I recently read that the average lifespan in this country is now eighty-one years of age for females and seventy six for males. Poor guys. But still, those figures are about ten years longer than it was when I was a little girl. Now I'm taking that number on faith, because I am certain those unnamed researchers have done their homework.

There are many reasons for this dramatic improvement in the lifespan of folks. I have already mentioned new healthcare technologies. Additionally, we are no longer a country of chain-smokers, most of us wear seatbelts, and a large number of our citizens have begun to watch what they eat and they have started to exercise regularly. But I believe the single largest factor in this extended life expectancy, the one thing that has had the biggest impact on the statistics, is that my mother can no longer practice medicine.

No, my mother was not a physician and she never went to medical school but she certainly didn't let that hold her back. A determined woman she was, and very smart – you could ask her and she would certainly tell you. She was the mother of three strong-willed girls and the wife of a man who gave her twenty dollars every Friday morning to buy groceries at the A&P store for the week. There wasn't a lot of money to go to the doctor and besides, my mother knew what she was doing. When we did have to seek outside medical care, it generally involved birth, death or the reattachment of something (like the day my father cut his finger off on a table saw). Most everything was handled at the kitchen sink and the more serious cases were remanded to the bathtub where peroxide was freely dispensed.

My mother actually had a medicine cabinet and one of the miracle cures in that cabinet was Merthiolate. You probably remember the stuff I'm talking about, because I'll bet your sainted mother used it in her practice as well. It was a topical antiseptic that was applied to every kid in the neighborhood that fell off their bike. They were covered with that stuff – it was put on every little spot that looked like it was bleeding. It was a dark red liquid that came in a little glass bottle. It smelled like a tire fire at the dump and it burned. Whoever was applying it would say, "It won't burn for long, just blow on it." There was (and I'm not kidding you) a skull and crossbones right there on the label!

I am not exactly sure what was in Merthiolate but I can promise you that I was the recipient of several major bicycle wrecks during the course of my childhood and they were all treated with Merthiolate and not a single one ever got infected, and they all healed up, well mostly. Once my knee didn't do so good so she brought in her backup medication – turpentine! That worked and my theory on why, is that once the bacteria got a gander at my mother approaching with that little green bottle of turpentine, those germs would flee the wound like rats deserting a sinking ship.

Whenever there was a fussy baby or a child with the croup, my mother would reach for another chemical marvel – paregoric. *Great stuff!* For any of you unfamiliar with this mystical substance, it was opium dissolved in alcohol. No, my mother was not a drug dealer or a crime lord with a street name like "Cash Momma" or "Mad Mattie" but if she had been she would have had more than twenty dollars to spend at the grocery store, I promise you.

You could buy paregoric back then without a prescription at any drugstore, and it was the reason why children used to behave better then than they do now. Basically, I spent the first ten years of my life very mellow and laid back, *and the next trying to get that monkey off my back.* There are photos in the family album of my sisters and me trying to sell our toys in an attempt to raise some quick paregoric cash. Every now and then I'll still fake a touch of the colic, just in case someone's mother has a bottle of the stuff tucked back for emergencies.

There were other standbys in my mother's cabinet of medical necessities. There were aspirin, which would cure everything from head lice to athlete's foot. There were Band-Aids, the standard dressing for anything short of a bullet wound. There were sewing needles and tweezers, my mother's tool of choice for splinter removal and for the extraction of foreign objects from nasal passages and ear canals. There was Vicks Vap-o-Rub, that mentholated miracle ointment that no doubt kept us all alive each winter when she warmed it and rubbed it on our chest and then covered us with a piece of my dad's old flannel shirt.

There was asphidity which was put into a small bag and was pinned to my slip or undershirt anytime someone sneezed or coughed around me. Now if you are completely unaware of asphidity, it is some concoction that smells *terribly* different than anything you've ever experienced. No comparison between it and the tire fire. It's a mixture of herbs, turpentine and tobacco that wards off the flu, polio, typhoid, rheumatic fever, whooping cough and any other malady known to mankind.

Finally, there was castor oil. If you've never enjoyed that semi-annual ritual for colon cleansing, then you haven't lived in the south.

I have heard a great deal of talk about healthcare these days but I don't pay very much attention to it. Once you have been treated by my mother's home healthcare and survived, everything else looks pretty darn good.

14

Hospital
Tips

My husband, Charlie, was in the hospital several times over the past few years of his life and each time we were admitted, we were given a booklet that claimed to tell us all we needed to know for a successful outing in the world of modern medical care. I nearly had it memorized as I read it out of boredom each time. Charlie wanted nothing to do with it, so it became my job to make sure the information was completely read and we were knowledgeable.

The booklet featured a smiling little character navigating various obstacles on the path back to good health. Occasionally this perky little fellow would look toward me and wink as he made a cogent point. I felt like I knew him – like we were old pals, and in our twelve short pages together, I grew to trust him. The pamphlet was upbeat and instructive, helpful, educational and by the last page, my friend was wearing lederhosen and a feathered cap while walking his little dog. We were eager to get on with the procedure that awaited him after being so well informed.

Unfortunately, we discovered during the recovery period that there were areas where more information was required. I don't believe that we were misled, you understand, although no one ever gave us a dog or a fedora. Rather, the pamphlet may have just skimmed areas where it should have delved more deeply, or perhaps some of the pages were just missing. To address these unintentional lapses, I have jotted down some observations about our hospital stay and Charlie's recovery. Hopefully, the following tips will prove useful should you or your loved ones require hospitalization.

Avoid words such as "rank" or "foul" while discussing hospital food with anyone from the nutrition department. The menu can get worse, I promise. In some form or fashion you should mark any uneaten food so they cannot slip it back onto your tray the next day. Do not eat sugar free anything that is placed on the tray – it's bad, really bad.

Go ahead and remove all articles of clothing in the lobby at check-in and let everyone get a good look. Front, rear and profile views. This will save a lot of time later on and will serve as an icebreaker with the entire hospital staff. They are going to see it all sooner or later so just get it over with.

Escape attempts are futile. The windows will only open two inches and it is impossible to blend in with departing visitors while wearing a backless hospital gown and pushing an IV trolley.

As a professional courtesy, do not refer to the night nurse as the "morphine fairy" after you've had surgery.

The statement "you will feel a little stick" translates into "grab the bedrail and hold on tight". Never forget that nursing students practice their craft by giving shots to oranges and that fruit cannot scream.

The correct answer to "Have you had a bowel movement?" is yes. There is no other answer. There should be no other words uttered. Just say "yes". It is a little known fact that the ancient Romans used to offer enemas as an alternative to beheading, and that three out of four victims chose beheading.

Do not point out issues of technique to your surgeon when he comes to see you after the surgery – just turn off the notebook computer that you have tuned to WebMD and set it aside. He went to school for a long, long time and does not want your advice.

No one actually knows why your blood has to be drawn from your body at 3:00 a.m., so do not ask. It is simply an absolute, like gravity or the speed of light. Also remember that the person from the lab is sleepy and this is their second job and that it is dark in your room, so make allowances if it takes eight or ten attempts to hit a vein.

Before signing it, savor the irony of the form that begins with the phrase, "Medicine is not an exact science." Be sure to note the section on page two where they quote the odds concerning your survival. Be attentive if you notice your doctor betting against rather than for. He is privy to inside information, and it may be time to rethink the procedure. Or at least have your spouse visit the ATM in the lobby in order to wager on the outcome if the odds go long.

Anything involving surgical gloves is not going to be good. If you find yourself thinking that a procedure wasn't so bad, then they are not finished. If your spouse is asked to step out of the room for a moment, grab her legs and whatever you do - do not let her go. The really bad stuff is about to take place and they do not want any witnesses.

Even if the additional cost for a private room is a million dollars, just pay it or at least tell them you will.

Comfortable beds are bad for you and as such, are prohibited by the AMA. Blankets thicker than tissue paper impede the circulation in your legs and are not available. Your bed was not short-sheeted by housekeeping as a prank. The sheets are just too short.

The thermostat on the wall is a placebo.

"Stat" is the medical term for "Get your ass down here right now!!" If you hear your nurse say it right after she takes your blood pressure or listens to your heart, you should start to worry.

Deny everything you said under anesthesia.

The urinary catheter tube only appears to be two inches in diameter. It is actually not much more than half an inch and should go right on in.

Threatening the lives of medical personnel is a felony in many states. Obtain legal counsel if you are unsure of the statutes in your area.

So, there you have it. Remember that your hospital stay is in many ways the barometer of your recovery period and that you may actually get well once you go home. Before long, you too can be walking the dog while wearing your recovery lederhosen and feathered fedora.

15

BOGO!

(Buy one get one free isn't always such a good thing)

In our area of the country, as you know, when we hear that someone has passed away we drop our head in a prayerful manner and quietly express our sympathy. That's just what we do.

I was seated next to a lady on an airplane a few years ago and she was probably 70 years of age. We began to chat and she told me she was going to New York City to visit her sister. I asked, "How many siblings do you have?"

She replied, "There were eight of us but one sister died so now there are only seven of us." We both dropped our heads prayerfully as she told me of her sister's passing.

"I'm so sorry, when did she die?"

"1944."

We dropped our heads again and I said, "I am so sorry." It's just a sign of respect – no matter how much time has passed.

In the South, when someone dies or gets sick, we take food to the family. You can buy that food. Go to the deli or a local restaurant – you can get whatever you want. But in the South, you need to actually *make* the food. You can put that KFC fried chicken on your grandmother's platter and the women in the kitchen taking care of the food will know where it came from. It just works out that way.

I make only one thing – miniature cheese biscuits. They go with everything. Now my friend, Jayne - she takes a crockpot of "refrigerator soup". I know, because she brought it to me last year when Charlie passed away. She puts everything in the refrigerator in the crockpot the night before and the next morning she shows up with her husband following closely behind, carrying that four gallon crockpot of refrigerator soup.

A couple of years ago, a friend of ours became very ill. I went to the freezer to pull out a Ziploc bag of biscuits and there were none to be found. I was running late for a board meeting and asked Charlie if he'd mind running to Publix and pick up what I needed so I could make cheese biscuits when I got home around noon.

He responded that he didn't think he could do that. He wasn't sure he would get the right stuff, he hadn't read the newspaper, he hadn't showered and most importantly he hadn't even had his second cup of coffee - but he would be glad to do it when he went to pick up some lunch in a few hours. I told him that it was just a couple of ingredients; surely he could just run in and pick them up. "No one will notice you've not showered and it's only three miles away - please have your coffee and read the paper when you get back. You can go through the express lane. I'll give you an exact list and it won't take 15 minutes.

You must understand, I hate going to the grocery store, especially on Wednesday because it's senior citizen day and penny coupon day at Publix! And, I just simply hate going to the grocery store with anyone - but especially with Charlie. We would always take two carts because I don't care what things cost by the half ounce. I want to run down the aisles, grab what I need and rush out. I don't need to sample what they're serving in the deli where the little lady is cooking the recipe of the day, I don't need to hear about the butcher's trip to Alaska and I don't care what the buy one get one free is that day.

Well, I went to the board meeting with the assurance that he would pick up what I needed. I was back home in two hours only to enter an empty house. No Charlie, no cheese in the refrigerator, no butter, no eggs – nothing I needed to make my miniature cheese biscuits.

I called his cell phone to no avail. Of course not, because he always left it in the truck – I had already given him a list, he knew I was in a meeting and what was the point in carrying it around? He was retired and Delta wasn't calling him for a trip.

After about 30 minutes, just as I was dialing the grocery store to have him paged, I hear the truck pull into the garage. Here he comes, huffing and puffing up the steps into the kitchen. He had two plastic bags in each hand and more sacks hanging on his arms.

I asked where in the world he had been. He just glared at me as he placed the bags on the counter. He said, "I'll be back, there's more in the truck."

I looked into the first bag and there was no butter, no cheese, no flour. But there were two large bottles of vanilla flavoring, which I did not need because I still had five bottles that he had brought back from Mexico eight years ago. Doling out half a teaspoon of vanilla at a time can take a lifetime you understand.

Next I discovered two dozen eggs. I needed four eggs. Well, they had a special – BOGO!

I opened bag number three only to see two large cans of shortening. Bag number four also held two large cans of shortening. Oh my gosh! Twelve pounds of lard! I needed two tablespoons. We could fry enough fish for fifty people with all that lard.

In the bottom of the next bag was my grocery wish list. I made sure that I only listed exactly what I needed and I numbered the items so it wouldn't exceed ten, just so he could go through the express lane.

Now I need to tell you that Charlie was a smart, smart man. He flew jet airplanes his entire adult life. He had the highest overall four year average of any student when he graduated with honors from the University of Georgia. He was in the top of his class. He excelled at everything he did. Smart, I tell you.

But somewhere down the middle of the third aisle of the grocery store, he lost all common sense.

I needed two packs of shredded cheddar cheese – I got eight packs of shredded cheese.

I needed one small can of shortening - I got twelve pounds of shortening.

I needed one pound of butter – I got five pounds of butter.

I needed four eggs – I got two dozen eggs.

I needed five pounds of sugar – I got twenty pounds of sugar.

I needed two pounds of flour – I got ten pounds of flour.

Now I am a true believer in accepting things you cannot change. I also believe there are times that you just need to let things ride. But I also believe there are times when you just need to let loose on things because you just can't stand it anymore.

Well, I decided this was the time just to let things ride. After all, he did me a favor - I did ask him to go the grocery. Charlie came in again, plopping down more flour and sugar and said, "I'll be right back."

I went to my list that I had found in the bottom of the shortening bag so I could see what in the world could be left in the truck. It was whipping cream. A small half pint of whipping cream. I didn't need that quart size because if I just used it once, by the time I needed it again it would be bad. But I was certain with the last trip to the truck he would return with ten gallons of whipping cream. I was wrong. Two quarts – BOGO!

I just stared at him and he said, "Well, obviously they wouldn't let me through the express lane."

Three days later I went to the grocery store. The cashier said, "I think I checked Charlie out the other day."

I told her it was a possibility.

"Well, he said you were making some little cheese biscuits for a friend. It was an interesting order."

I replied, "Well, since you're from here you understand that anytime someone gets sick or a family member passes away (we both dropped our heads prayerfully at that point), I make miniature cheese biscuits. They're quick and easy and they just go with everything - soup or salad or breakfast. Any meal or just a snack. I usually make about two or three dozen so they can freeze what they don't use."

The cashier looked at me and exclaimed, "Oh my God, is there an epidemic?"

16

The Great
Garage Sale

A few months back I had a garage sale. That is just easier for me to say than, "I had a yard sale". I really needed to get rid of some things. Now you have to know that I moved into my new house in north Georgia from the Atlanta area just 18 months ago. *WOW!* You would have thought we lived at Buckingham Palace. No kidding! Two tractor trailers, 784 boxes, 13 rooms of furniture plus what was stored in the basement and upstairs in the attic. Apparently the moving company thought we were royalty, as well – at least according to the final tab. However, I digress. Back to the matter at hand.

This garage sale was awesome, I tell you. My dear cousin Louise and her husband, Bob, showed up to help me. Now understand these two sweet people had just helped me *unpack* boxes a few months earlier. We sat up tables and priced every single little thing. We organized and worked for several days like Trojans. I hated it but I certainly enjoyed the time we spent together and wouldn't take anything in the world for it. By the time we were finished, I felt like I was opening a Woolworth's Five and Dime Store.

Friday morning came early and before the day was over, I had a couple of thousand dollars in my pocket. I felt like I was on my way to becoming a big department store magnate. I couldn't wait to see how much I would make on Saturday! Until I actually figured out that the stuff I sold for $2,000.00 probably cost $10,000.00 over the many years spent collecting it. Still, somebody else is dusting it now, while I'm spending the $2,000.00 on satellite TV and streaming movies for a couple of months.

At the end of the day on Saturday, there were still plenty of items left for me to take to Goodwill. I had marked things down to $2.00, including an old turntable that would play records – you know "vinyl" – mine were just "records" because I had bought them so long ago that they were just "records". I did try to actually give a few things away. When you can't give things away for free, there's a problem. And it's not just strangers that won't take my stuff, my sons won't take my stuff! Almost everyone I talk to says the same thing: "None of the kids want my stuff".

"They don't want the dishes I got as a wedding present," my friends say. They don't want my grandmother's handkerchiefs or her embroidered dresser scarfs. They don't want the linens or rugs I've never used. They don't want the bookcases or the DVDs or the framed prints that used to hang on the walls. They don't want the nearly new sofa or the desks or even my china cabinet. Just put all that stuff in the casket with me because if you don't, my children will put it straight in the trash!

I have so much stuff and those boys don't have any idea what it's worth. Well, actually they probably do – it's worth nothing. If it can't fit on their cellphone or their iPad, they don't want it. They go out to eat or order pizza; what would they put in a china cabinet anyway? An empty pizza box? What would they do with a crystal decanter? Put craft beer in it? Go ahead – try to sell a silver plated coffee set and water pitcher. Together they're worth less than a cup of Starbuck's coffee in a paper cup. And when you think about it, they should be. Who would put coffee in a silver container? It would be cold in about three seconds. And the water pitcher would drop condensation all over that lovely polished furniture. When was the last time you used your silver service? Yet for years, they were all the rage as a priceless wedding present. Today's favorite wedding present is an envelope with a gift card in it.

I was talking with my friend who stopped by to visit on Sunday after the great estate sale and she had brought her two children with her. Like most teenagers they could care less about all the old stuff in the basement, until they found the records. You would have thought those kids had discovered gold.

"OMG! Look at the size of these things. It's like a Frisbee. Who is the Kingston Trio? You're kidding me, someone is actually named 'Petula'? If they're the Beach Boys, why aren't they wearing swim trunks? That's a funny title: 'The Buttoned Down Mind of Bob Newhart" – what kind of music is that?"

I would have liked to have listened to some of the records with those kids and shared a few laughs and told them how great Petula Clark actually sounded but my record player was on the $2.00 table and someone smarter than me has it now.

17

An Attempt
to Simplify

I like to keep a clean house. When my house is orderly, I feel better and I think better. I even breathe more easily in a clean house – it calms me. If someone were to drop by my house unannounced, most of the time the place would look pretty good. But, I do have a dirty little secret.

My jewelry boxes seem to always be a mess. I'm committed to a few pieces of jewelry so that I don't have to rummage through that mess and each night when I put things back in place, it's simple – it goes right back into that empty spot.

Isn't living in your own home supposed to be simple and easy? Well, not really – at least for me. Few things in my life require more intentionality than living a simple, edited life. Whether it's a hectic schedule during a time of remodeling, overflowing jewelry chests or the unchecked thoughts that can run through my mind, I need to be aggressive in my pursuit of simplicity if there is any hope of it being a reality.

Left to their own devices these seemingly small things have a way of spiraling out of control. And time after time, I learn that this is the very kind of work that is worth it. As painful as paring down can feel, there is nothing quite like the feeling of a lighter load, particularly when you can see in hindsight that you were never meant to carry all that stuff anyway.

Another thing that's tricky about simplifying your life is that you can't make just a one-time decision. This requires day-by-day, moment-by-moment deciding. Each time the mail comes it is easy to hold onto that "one important coupon" or when you run to the store just to pick up a loaf of bread there's a myriad of choices that present themselves to challenge this call to simplicity. Now don't get me wrong, I love abundance in many forms, but I am learning that it should not be at the cost of a sound mind or a peaceful home.

Living more simply is a personal thing. No one can tell you to do it and it doesn't just happen. There is no "one-size-fits-all" formula that is going to solve all your problems. Still, it only takes a couple of minutes of looking inward to have a pretty good sense of what areas in your life could use a little pruning. I intuitively know where my personal excesses lie. As much as I protest, I must listen to that knowing and throw off the dead weight. There really is something exhilarating to living life a little less encumbered.

So . . . I just spent two hours cleaning out my jewelry box and found a receipt from 1985 from the drug store! Downsizing and simplicity are not magic, but they are a little bit magical.

18

An Economy
of Words

Sometimes, Rodney — usually in a gentle way but a bit abrupt at other times — will tell me I'm taking too long to explain something. This doesn't happen often and never when he has time to enjoy a long story (you know, like when we're in the car) – but rather when he's in a bit of a rush or has something else he'd rather do.

"Can you give me the short version of this story? I really don't need all of that." I always think my stories are worth an investment of time and Rodney does normally, but not always.

I'll frown and say, "Yes, I can but it will be your loss because it's actually a very interesting story."

The Southern story telling version always includes who's kin to who, who was arrested, who went to jail, who was almost arrested, how long I've known them and then, usually, I veer off into a personal recollection of one of the other minor characters that I briefly mentioned. Perhaps I should tell you that Rodney's patience is tried when I am telling this kind of story over something simple such as how the bakery muffins weren't fresh at one grocery and how I had to tell the store manager, whom I've known for 20 years, then I went to another store where the muffins weren't any fresher but were almost double the price. Keep in mind that I included the history of the grocery store, what used to be on that spot of land, how I knew the store manager and the cost of milk.

Rodney will take a deep breath and ask nicely, "Did you get the muffins, Kathryn?"

"No."

I don't believe in "a few words" when "a lot of words" cost the same. First, I'm Irish and secondly, I'm Southern. I love to tell a tale, and also because I really like to get my money's worth, why wouldn't I want to use more than less? All the words are free. Why not use them?

I remember back last year, quite by accident, I discovered that economy of words can be quite effective.

I had flown to New York for a few days. On the flight up, I apparently picked up some bug and that lead to a sore throat and laryngitis. By the time I returned home a few days later, I had lost my voice. There was a drunk redneck on the plane back to Atlanta. I'm talking straight out of the backwoods, wearing a

John Deere baseball cap and a Lynyrd Skynyrd black T-shirt.

Unfortunately, there were no seats in the first-class section and I was in coach – you know, the back of the bus with all the other tourists – the cheap seats.

This redneck guy was sitting behind me on the opposite side, slumping over and slurring words he used loudly. About thirty minutes into the trip, I got up, passed his seat, and went to the tiny bathroom in the back of the plane. In seconds, someone was jerking the door, and pulling with great might and clatter, making all amounts of noise until I opened the door. I'm thinking, where are the flight attendants? Only two on board the plane it seemed and of course, they were taking care of the people at the front – you know, first class. Let steerage deal with steerage, I am certain this is what they think. They don't want to go back there either.

Well, anyway, the drunk in the Lynyrd Skynyrd T-shirt was standing face to face with me. "Oh, ma'am! I'm sorry! I didn't know you was in there." My first thought was, "That didn't occur to you when the door was locked and the lighted sign said 'Occupied'?!!" But since I really had no voice and as a retiree using one of my few remaining privileges with the airline, I said nothing but simply stared at him and moved away in disgust. I waved away his words and shook my head. When the plane landed, I thought, "Good! This flight is finally over and I do not have to listen to that jerk any longer. I can get away from him."

As I have done for more than twenty-five years, I was one of the last to deplane. Taking my time, I walked at a slow pace to the train that would take me to the main departure terminal. There were five cars on the train and wouldn't you know that I picked the one with the same drunk on it? He began his blubbering apology again about the bathroom door.

The only thing worse than a crying drunk is a sorry drunk. And I don't mean that in the Southern way of being "sorry-no-account." I mean one who is apologizing.

But since I couldn't really speak and did not want to speak with this guy, it made it very easy to ignore him. Again, I waved away his apology and, unsmiling, just shook my head. He turned away finally with a few grumbling words. Great! Just fine. I think I was finally able to get rid of him and put him in his place.

I'm now thinking that Rodney is right. Sometimes fewer words may be better.

19

Remembering 9-11-2001

September 11, 2001

My story of the events on September 11th are not any different than several hundred pilot spouses that had their husbands or wives in the air that day.

My husband, Charlie, was the Captain of Delta Flight #71 from Rome, Italy, to Atlanta on that day. He had left Atlanta on September 9th on his weekly trip to Europe. On the morning of September 11th about 8:55 I received a telephone call as I was having coffee and reading the morning newspaper; it was from our CPA. After I said, "Hello," he immediately asked, "Is Charlie at home?"

"No, he's in Rome and will be back this afternoon," I told him.

"Kathryn, you need to turn on the television to CNN."

I reached for the television remote and as the picture appeared, I heard the voice on the other end exclaim, "Oh, my God!" just as I saw a plane explode into one of the Twin Towers. My heart sank in disbelief.

My other telephone lined beeped in. It was our daughter, Leah. As I answered she asked if I had heard any news. The other telephone line rang and it was our nephew, a radio announcer/ newscaster from Vidalia, asking if Charlie was at home – he had received a wire at the radio station about planes crashing in New York.

The phone rang once again – this time the name on the Caller ID Box was "Delta Air Lines". As I picked up the phone, I took a deep breath. At this point I knew nothing except planes were exploding. It was the International Assistant Chief Pilot Dick Cassel for Delta.

"Kathryn, Charlie's all right," were his immediate words.

I knew Charlie had left Rome several hours earlier (there's an eight-hour time difference and it's a 12-hour flight to Atlanta). He told me Delta was turning some of the planes back to their original departure points in Europe but there had been some problems with the airports in Rome & Athens and they were not turning those flights back; but they were "going to put him down on the first piece of land we can find".

I thanked him for his call and then asked for some additional reassurance. "Dick, our son David is in the air. He's on American from Madrid. I don't know if he's going straight to DFW or if he's coming through Kennedy. I don't know his flight number."

David was a 767 International First Officer for American Airlines at the time. He & his wife were supposed to be on the flight from Madrid, Spain to the U.S. He oftentimes flies a route from European destinations to JFK/New York and then "deadheads" to his home base in Dallas, Texas.

Just as Dick told me he would check on the American flight and keep me posted on both, my door opened and in walked my Leah and 6-year-old granddaughter, Madison. I needed them both that day.

Our youngest son, Stephen, was in the DeKalb County Fire Academy and the officers there had him calling every 30 minutes to check on things. Although he had been put on alert status as emergency personnel, DeKalb County did offer to let him be released from class if he were needed at home. We knew we were safe; it was the people in the air and around Hartsfield we didn't know about. If needed, he could help them more than us.

Throughout the day, we listened intently to the news. We watched over and over the fiery crashes of the Boeing airplanes; we answered the door; we took phone calls; and, we prayed a lot. We were in constant contact with our other son, Doug, as well as other family members.

Delta offered to send someone out to the house to stay with us; they kept us informed throughout the day to try and help ease our worst fears. Finally, late in the afternoon, the call came that Charlie was to land in Bermuda. We had learned earlier that David arrived safely at home in Dallas.

Charlie was one of the two Delta flights that landed in Bermuda that day. He was fortunate; he didn't have to spend three days on the airplane as many crewmembers did when they didn't have enough housing in Halifax.

But more than fortunate, he was blessed that he came home. When he arrived in Atlanta, he was the second flight into Hartsfield after it re-opened.

When he walked in the door at home, tears ran down his face as he told us of F-16 escorting him into Atlanta and of the ground people that lined up on the runway holding signs and welcoming him back and of the airline personnel lining the jetway and down the concourses holding signs and giving away Hershey's silver kisses to the crew as they cheered their safe arrival.

My husband has recently retired (FAA mandates retirement at age 60) after more than 32 years with Delta. This is an experience we will remember and always be thankful he survived.

20

The Deconstruction of the American Male

There used to be television shows that celebrated dads: *"Father Knows Best", "Leave It to Beaver", "Bonanza", "Little House on the Prairie"* and even *"The Waltons".* The fathers in these programs supported their families and loved their children and wives. Even into the 1980s with *"Family Ties",* fathers were cast in a positive light.

But since then, fathers have become television's punching bags. Advertisements portray them as buffoons – so inept they couldn't change a light bulb. Popular sitcoms and cartoons make dads look like bumbling, clueless slobs.

Children's books like *Berenstain Bear* make Mama Bear the fount of wisdom and Poppa Bear is more a child than a father.

For the past 20 or 25 years, manhood has come under attack in universities and even major corporations. I think that to be a male, and particularly a white male, in today's world is to belong to the "patriarchy". Years ago before things were so "feminine" – patriarchy was described as a society where the male held control and made all the rules and women stayed home and cared for the children. However, in today's world it is quite the contrary – patriarchy is used to describe an unjust social system that discriminates against women.

Our culture - our embrace in some instances - of extreme feminism and the errant behavior of some men have diminished the old ideals of fatherhood – a certain amount of stoicism and grit, provider for the family, defender of his wife and children.

This diminution of manhood is an attack on the family itself. By undermining the role of the father, the importance of the family as a basic building block of culture and society shrinks.

The fact that a father and a mother bring different skills to raising a child, and that the father plays an important part in the childhood development, should be obvious to anyone – whether or not you have children.

Many years ago I watched a segment on "60 Minutes". The researchers went to a neighborhood playground and filmed parents and children at the slide. The moms all held the children's hands, they offered to go down the slide with them, they cajoled them and finally allowed their child to climb back down the ladder. The dads stood at the bottom of the slide shouting encouragement, clapping their hands and insisting the child come on down by themselves.

Men more often teach strength and, in that strength, comes leadership. How do we continue to teach strength if males are constantly belittled?

I think that first we should stop the attacks on manhood. I've heard many women slam their husbands or boyfriends, or men in general, with chauvinistic remarks as pointed and stereotypical of any attributed to men when "male chauvinism" came under fire more than 50 years ago. Those assaults should stop. Why can't women respect and honor the person they supposedly love and stop making comments about men they don't even know? They are not all alike.

We can quit listening to and using the language of academics who want to feminize men and who want to make ordinary male behavior toxic. We can reject theories that claim no differences exist between men and women and we can celebrate those differences.

We should express our appreciation of the good fathers that we see around us – those good fathers that raised us. I was blessed with a loving, caring father as a child and that continued until the day he died. I would disagree over the years with many of his decisions but I learned as I grew older that the decisions he made were made with love. Some people grew up with a deadbeat dad that deserted his family or was cruel, hardhearted or a drunkard.

Whatever the case, we can see fathers around us who love their wives and children, who get up and go to work every morning to provide for them, who offer their children guidance into adulthood both by word and by example. A good number of men fit that description.

So even if you grew up under the thumb of a terrible father, you can find someone to emulate in the men around you. For single moms with sons, finding a role model is important and can be difficult – unless of course you were as fortunate as me and had a great dad as a role model for your son.

Right now we are going through tough times in our country. When I watch the rioters and looters on the news, I notice their youth and I would guess the majority of them grew up without the influence of a strong, good father to teach them right from wrong.

My father was a strong, productive, protective, caring man. We were taught to respect him by my mother –not only because he was the head of the household and our father, but because of his actions. He earned our respect with all he did – not only for his family but for his community and his friends. I hope to honor him by acts of remembrance.

I call on my sons, all of whom are fathers themselves, and ask that you honor your family and your friends by earning the respect of your wives and your children and those that love you.

21

I'm So Sorry You're Hurting

In My Defense I'm Not Perfect & Never Claimed to Be

I have learned over the years that it is not uncommon for parents and children to experience difficult relationships, and these relationships can certainly affect the well-being of the parent and child. Actually, the statistics reflect that one adult child in ten is incommunicado with either their mother or father, while other studies, such as the one done by Rin Reczek, a sociology professor at the Ohio State University, show that the actual number is one in four adult children are estranged from their parents.

Some people criticize Sigmund Freud for his emphasis on the role of the mother in his psychoanalytic theories. Freud's theories often highlighted the significance of early childhood experiences in shaping an individual's psyche.

Critics argue that Freud's focus on the mother as a source of psychological issues can oversimplify complex human behavior and place undue blame on their mothers. *(Just wondering if it all goes back to the fact that the mother brought that little booger into the world!)* Freud's theories have been both influential and controversial, and they have sparked ongoing debate and reinterpretation within the field of psychology for decades.

Constantly blaming a parent for all of your problems may be a sign of an underlying issue. Perhaps you should reflect on what you can change in your own life and how to improve it rather than placing constant blame on someone else. Look within. As the saying goes, "You shouldn't throw stones if you live in a glass house". This might actually help to improve family relationships altogether.

Mothers always seem to catch the flack. Sometimes we just get tired of it – so my best piece of advice for grown children is simple: Toughen up Buttercup. The world is a tough place. Be responsible for your actions. Stop blaming people.

22

Art History of the Wiener Dog

Although seldom discussed in the writings of most art historians, the wiener dog (or dachshund, as at least twelve people still insist on calling it) was intermittently a favorite subject of many artists, including several of the Great Masters (although this remains controversial). In fact, throughout the history of mankind, the wiener dog has often been utilized as a symbol for many of our human traits: love, war, hunger, greed, fear, hypochondria and swollen glands, just to name a few of the more common ones.

The fear of wiener dogs, littlelongdogophobia, for example, was most prevalent in Mesopotamia around 500 B.C. and the art from this time reflected that culture's anxiety toward this little animal. Other societies, however, revered the canine, although we know little of these people since their civilizations lasted on average only three to five weeks.

Why the wiener dog has found its way into our hearts and

minds, and ultimately our culture, is difficult to say. We know only that, somehow, this small sausage-shaped animal with its shrill, high pitched bark and sometimes neurotic behavior has touched something we recognize deep inside ourselves.

23

Beyond
the Clouds

There are cracks in the sidewalk with stubborn little patches of grass sticking through them. Most of the stores were boarded up. A fall breeze came up and blew some leaves lightly against the cracked plate glass window. The front door of her father's mercantile store opened and she saw him for the first time. At eighteen, she watched him carefully as he walked towards her.

His square frame filled his olive drab Army uniform. His auburn hair a bit windblown and his face sprinkled with freckles.

It wasn't the color of his blue grey eyes that took her breath away - it was what was inside them. They were the color of the stormy sky that would drown you in the rain. Without a word, she knew she would love him forever.

Death would come, as it always does. No matter the age, it's always too soon.

His came on a rainy night in May. The year was 1932. He left her as quickly as he had appeared in her father's store in the little village in northern England.

A neighbor's boy was finding his way home on his bicycle in the early evening. As they met on the bridge the car swerved and slammed into the rock wall.

The rain continued to fall as the local authorities knocked on the door of their modest home. Their young son ran upstairs for his mother. Throughout the night the mother and son cradled one another in each other's arms.

Spring came early the following year. It seemed the entire village, as most of the country, had been battling some form of illness. Kate, now the owner of her father's store, was stricken with influenza.

She found peace in her final days, knowing her mother would take loving care of their son and that she would once again look deeply into the blue grey eyes of her husband – if not in this world then in another.

24

The Last Time

Today I am thinking of "last times" – the last time I spent Mother's Day with my mother, the last time I helped my dad in the chicken house and we made a Chinese checker board, the last time I saw my husband smile at me.

Our time may be short or it may be long here and our memories, of course, will come in all sizes and flavors. So if there is anything I would leave as a lasting thought when my life is over, it probably would be that you make long and lasting friendships and that you build rich, full and great memories, while you are here on this earth, because when your "last time" comes your cup will then be full.

Alfred D. Souza said, *"For a long time it had seemed to me that life was about to begin – real life. But there was always some obstacle in the way, something to be gotten through first, some unfinished business, time still to be served, a debt to be paid. Then life would begin. At last it dawned on me that these obstacles were my life."*

When you have your "last time" moment, as we all will, you may come to the same place that Souza came to — that life is in the *here and now*. As I said, the "last time" with people I loved has given me time to reflect and it can be a little scary or it can be a gift. I choose the latter. In the big scheme of things we are always in transition. My "last time" is really the opening of a door to a "first time" on the new path that lies ahead. I'm looking forward to it!

The reference to the chicken house needs a bit of explanation to strangers. There were actual chicken houses behind my parents' home but over the years my father turned them into storage buildings – places he kept his prized possessions, where he spent hours with his friends and where he did his work wooding. There were no chickens – but to family, they are still remembered as "chicken houses".

25

Death and Heartache

"Death leaves a heartache no one can heal,

Love leaves a memory no one can steal."

July 21, 1942 – January 3, 2016

26

Reincarnation

When we open up and allow our soul's memory to emerge and express itself, we can be amazed at the multiple personalities each one of us may have. I don't mean multiple personalities in the sense of a psychological disorder. I mean each of us has had multiple experiences in past lifetimes that allow us to have memories and intuitions that can't be explained any other way.

I know and recognize streets when I've visited other countries or cities that I have not been to in this lifetime. I recognize certain people; I can look into their eyes because they have not changed. I know another's touch; I realize it when they reach out to me. I feel what's in someone else's heart when we speak of certain things. Imagines often flood my brain and stay with me for days. I have felt the love of someone from my past; when I have met them for the first time in this lifetime, my heart races and I long for their return; I have missed them because they were once part of me. I often hear someone call my name in the distance but I cannot see a face.

If you believe in karma, reincarnation of the soul is unequaled. "For whatever a man sows that shall he also reap." This means to me that every human soul is in control of his or her destiny, depending on what that person needs to work on the next time around. The soul lives on and the learning of self continues.

27

Fate & Destiny

Today is a very special day for me. It was two years ago today that I felt absolutely complete in this life. While my life has truly been wonderful, I always knew there was something just a bit more – something from my past that haunted me always.

A reunion of heart and souls in the world today can be very complicated and complex. While we can never go back in time, our soul goes on forever. How wonderful if we were to have another lifetime together – but we do not have that control. It is left to fate and destiny.

What I do appreciate is that I had one more time to look into those blue grey eyes and to tell him how much I love him. How much I've always loved him and how much I will always miss him. No matter what life it is.

Rin was born in 1889 in England. He fought in World War I during the year 1917. Death came in May 1932, when he ran into a rock wall of a bridge while avoiding a young boy.

He was married to Kate and they had a son whose name I do not know in this life. Sad, I know, but we aren't supposed to recall all of the events of a previous life.

Details of past lives together are very clear at times and the feelings of love are like the first time – when I met him in my father's mercantile store.

Throughout most days of our life, we have chance encounters with people, or situations that can be and often are life transforming. If you think about it, your life is sprinkled with such transformational chance encounters that you never would have imagined.

A chance encounter is the ultimate serendipity, an accident of happy coincidence or good fortune. Such encounters do not occur every day, but they do happen. And yes, they have the capacity to completely transform or alter your life. Take advantage of them and know they have meaning because they may not ever present themselves again.

This book is dedicated to Eve Oldham.

A woman that continues to amaze, support,

inspire, create and bring light to every day.

Her tenacity and perseverance are beyond belief.

Thank you for your friendship.

Made in the USA
Middletown, DE
13 April 2024

52858026R10075